Dear Primrose,
May you know that you <u>don't</u>
have to 'fit in' to have good
friends! Be yourself!
Elaine
Slade
x

Copyright © 2022 Slade Books.

www.elainesladebooks.com

elaine@elainesladebooks.com

The right of Elaine Slade to be identified as the author and Monika Dzikowicz as the illustrator of this work has been asserted by them in accordance with the Copyright, Designs and Patents Act 1988.

All rights reserved. No part of this publication may be reproduced, stored in a retrieval system, or transmitted in any other form or by any means, electronic, mechanical, photocopying, recording or otherwise, without the prior written permission of Slade Books.

ISBN: 978-1-8384003-4-7

A CIP catalogue record for this book is available from the British Library.

BOZ PUBLICATIONS

First published by Boz Publications Ltd 2022

Boz Publications Ltd.

71-75 Shelton Street, Covent Garden, London WC2H 9JQ

office@bozpublications.com - www.bozpublications.com

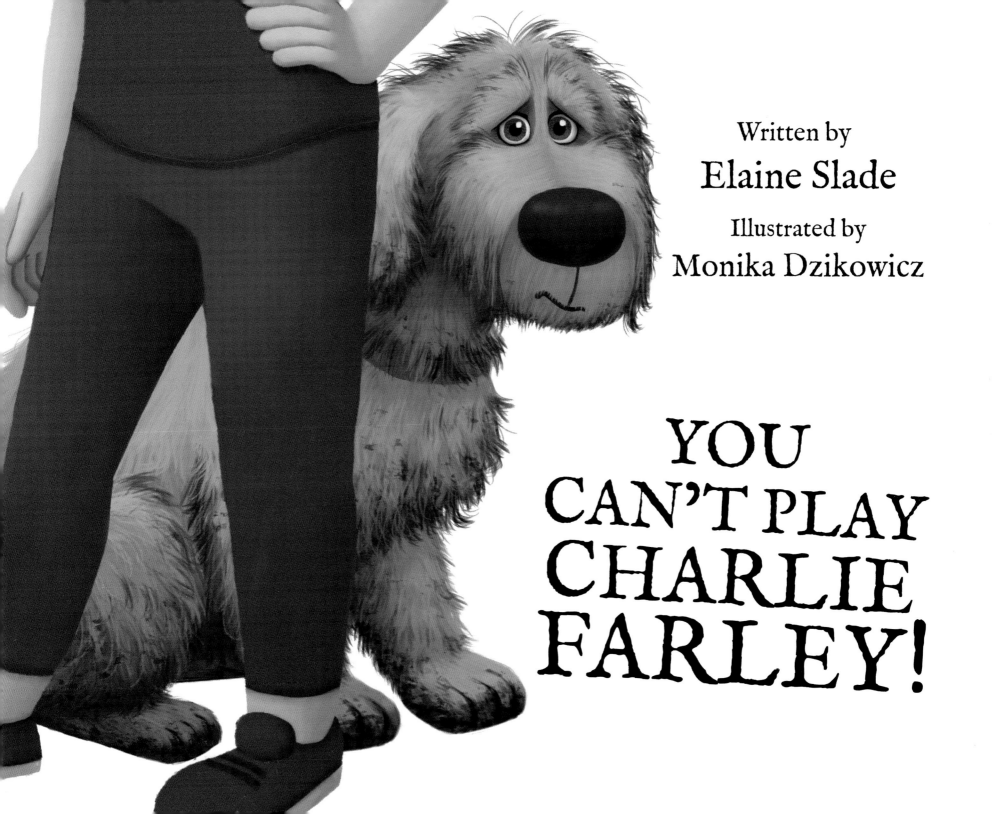

Written by
Elaine Slade

Illustrated by
Monika Dzikowicz

YOU CAN'T PLAY CHARLIE FARLEY!

Jasper attracted admiration and fame,
everywhere he trotted, dogs knew his name.

He looked just like a Goldendoodle,
he fitted in, had full approval.

Charlie Farley, always anxious to fit in,
Jasper's friends exchange a knowing grin.

He did not look like a Goldendoodle,
if he tried to engage, off dogs would toodle.

NO!

YOU
CAN'T PLAY
CHARLIE FARLEY!

Whereas Jasper was admired by Goldendoodles,
Charlie Farley had to beg a posse of Poodles.

"My Dad is a Poodle
just like you,
Can I enrol
in your club too?"

NO! YOU CAN'T PLAY CHARLIE FARLEY!

As Jasper raised his head and puffed up tall,
Charlie Farley appealed to Retrievers tossing a ball.

"My Mum is a Retriever just like you,
Can I join in your game too?"

YOU CAN'T PLAY
CHARLIE FARLEY!

Whilst Jasper paraded and held his own,
Charlie Farley wandered alone.

He moaned and groaned,
why didn't he fit?
It shouldn't matter
about looks, should it?

Around the corner,
who should he see?

Dappled brown dog,
crouched by a tree.

"The other dogs
say I can't play,
However hard I try,
they scamper away."

NO!
YOU
CAN'T PLAY
MINNIE WINNIE!

An idea came with a FLASH and a BANG!

"*We can play together!*"
Charlie sang.

What games they played,

what fun they had.

Other lonely dogs joined,
no longer sad!

YES! YOU CAN PLAY CHARLIE FARLEY!

Jasper and Charlie Farley were brothers.
Whilst one fitted in, the other belonged.
Charlie Farley had learned to be himself,
set free to be a friend for someone else.

Have you ever heard the words 'YOU can't play'?
Be yourself, find someone lonely to whom you can say
'You CAN play!'

Draw your game together here.

CHARLIE FACE MASK

JASPER FACE MASK

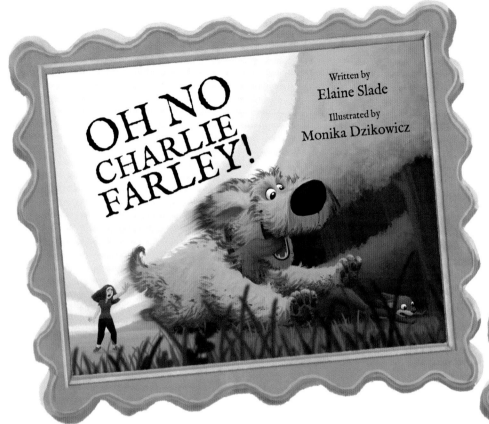

Written by
Elaine Slade

Illustrated by
Monika Dzikowicz

LOOK!
MORE EXCITING CHARLIE FARLEY ADVENTURES.

Written by
Elaine Slade

Illustrated by
Monika Dzikowicz

AVAILABLE AT:

www.elainesladebooks.com

www.bozpublications.com

This story will have a specific purpose as a tool
to support children through the personal loss of a person or a pet.

Why did Kami die? Was she not coming back?
Saying goodbye to Kami took Charlie aback.
Jasper explained,
*"Her death's hard to accept although it's true,
I'm really going to miss her too."*

IT'S OKAY
TO FEEL SAD
CHARLIE FARLEY!

ANOTHER
STORY
COMING
SOON!

CHARLIE'S ACTIVITY GUIDE!
- Helping children explore genuine friendship and celebrate differences -

Complete the page, *Have you ever heard the words "You can't play"?* together.
Support your child/ren sensitively if they want to talk about friendships that they find difficult.

Photocopy the mask templates, cut out, attach string or elastic and use them to act out the story.

Extension of mask activity with older children; explore how Charlie and Jasper felt at different points in the story.
Sensitively ask questions such as *Why didn't you stick up for me, Jasper?*

Create a *What makes a good friend?* poster.
Draw two friends in the middle and add phrases around them to describe true friendship.

Draw a central line on a piece of paper, write GOOD FRIEND / NOT A GOOD FRIEND.
Discuss what to write on either side, keep the negative side mild with young children e.g. *Wants you to play their games all the time.*

Hot seat Charlie or Jasper or Minnie; one of you pretends to be a character, others ask them questions related to the story
e.g. To Charlie - what lesson did you learn by the end of the story? To Minnie - how did you feel when Charlie played with you?

Look at words in the story that your child might not have understood e.g. enrol, posse, paraded, dappled, appealed.
Look up the meaning together.

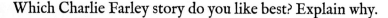

Write or verbally tell a story about two children/animals becoming friends together.

Draw and cut out a paper chain of people from folded paper and make them all different; write FRIENDS along the chain.

Which Charlie Farley story do you like best? Explain why.

JASPER'S MESSAGE TO PARENTS AND TEACHERS.

Before reading the book:

- Who can you see on the front cover?
- I wonder why Charlie Farley is behind his owner's legs? What do you think?
- Does the blurb on the back cover tell us any more about the story?
- Do you think Charlie Farley will find some friends? If so, how?

Whilst reading the book:

- Can you help me find the little squirrel as we turn over each page?
- Encourage your child/ren to join in sadly *NO! You can't play Charlie Farley!* and then a loud and happy *YES! You CAN...*
- *Jasper attracted admiration and fame.* Where is the story set? How do you know? Do you recognise any of the characters?
- *Charlie Farley, always anxious to fit in.* Which word describes how Charlie Farley is feeling?
- *NO! You can't play Charlie Farley!* How many times did Charlie hear those words? Did Jasper have the same trouble?
- *He moaned and groaned...* Why is Charlie looking at himself in the puddle? What is the problem?
- *Around the corner...* Why was Minnie on her own? How was she feeling? Who else feels like that in the story?
- *"We can play together!"* How do we know that Charlie and Minnie were happy now?
- *Other lonely dogs...* Why did other dogs come and play? Can you find the words which show us how they were feeling?
- Which part of the story did you like best? Why was that?

Questions to help explore genuine friendship and celebrate our differences:

- Can you think of another Charlie Farley story which starts with others being cross with him?
- How does this story begin? How does it end? How does it change?
- Have you ever felt like Charlie OR Jasper? What did you do? What could you do next time?
- Recall the special and unique theme of *Oh No Charlie Farley!* and talk about the importance of being yourself and knowing your own self-worth in friendship.

Elaine Slade - Author

Elaine is a former Deputy Head who loves exploring a good story and inspiring children, including her family (four daughters, two granddaughters), to love reading. She is passionate about raising children's self-esteem and knowing their own worth. Growing up, Elaine realised she needed to be herself and befriend others rather than trying to fit in to group expectations to make friends, just like Charlie Farley.

www.elainesladebooks.com

Monika Dzikowicz - Illustrator

Monika, just like Charlie Farley, spent most of her childhood covered in mud; frolicking in nature; and looking up to her cool, older sister. When she grew up she embraced her uniqueness and became an illustrator who strives to visualise stories, which empower people and teach them emotional intelligence.

www.monikadzikowicz.com

And meet the REAL
Charlie Farley and Jasper.

For the Nkosi family, Izwe, Anne,
Zoë and Phoebe, great role models
of belonging together whilst
embracing and respecting their
UNIQUENESS!
Elaine x

THANK YOU TO MY FAMILY AND FRIENDS
FOR LOVING ME THE WAY I AM
AND FOR MAKING ME FEEL LIKE i BELONG.
♡ MONIKA